Mrs. Wishy-Washy and the Big Wash

HAMERAY
PUBLISHING GROUP

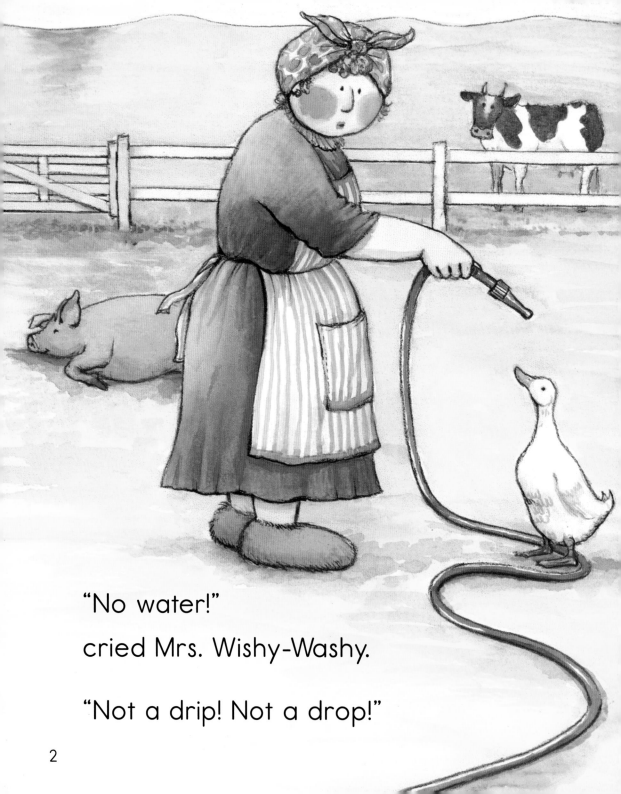

"No water!"
cried Mrs. Wishy-Washy.

"Not a drip! Not a drop!"

2

The animals laughed
their dusty laugh.

Hooray! Hooray!
No washing today!

Mrs. Wishy-Washy said,
"We must go to town
and look for water.
Get on the truck!"

The cow, the pig, and the duck
got on the back of the truck.

Away they went to town
to look for water.

They came to the book store.

"No water in the book store,"
said Mrs. Wishy-Washy.

They came to the music store.

"No water in the music store,"
said Mrs. Wishy-Washy.

7

Then they came to
the cake shop.

"Cakes!" mooed the cow.

"I'm hungry!" squealed the pig.

"Stop! Stop! Stop!"
quacked the duck.

"No, no, no!"
said Mrs. Wishy-Washy.

"We must look for water
for a wash."

At last they came to a car wash.

"This is it!"
said Mrs. Wishy-Washy.
"In we go!"

The truck went into
the car wash.

Splash, splash
went the soapy water.

"That is cold!"
squealed the pig.

Swish, swish went the brushes.

"That tickles!" mooed the cow.

Woosh, woosh went the air.

"My feathers!" quacked the duck.

The truck came out of
the car wash.

Mrs. Wishy-Washy smiled.

"You look so clean!
You smell so sweet!
We'll go back to the
cake shop for a treat."

Pink cakes! Yellow cakes!
Green! Oh bliss!

Thank you, Mrs. Wishy-Washy!
Here is a kiss!